FISHY RIDDLES

FISHY RIDDLES

by Katy Hall
and Lisa Eisenberg

pictures by
Simms Taback

PUFFIN BOOKS

PUFFIN BOOKS
Published by the Penguin Group
Penguin Books USA Inc., 375 Hudson Street, New York, New York 10014, U.S.A.
Penguin Books Ltd, 27 Wrights Lane, London W8 5TZ, England
Penguin Books Australia Ltd, Ringwood, Victoria, Australia
Penguin Books Canada Ltd, 10 Alcorn Avenue, Toronto, Ontario, Canada M4V 3B2
Penguin Books (N.Z.) Ltd, 182–190 Wairau Road, Auckland 10, New Zealand

Penguin Books Ltd, Registered Offices: Harmondsworth, Middlesex, England

First published in the United States of America by Dial Books for Young Readers, 1983
Published in a Puffin Easy-to-Read edition, 1993

9 10

LIBRARY OF CONGRESS CATALOGING-IN-PUBLICATION DATA

Hall, Katy.
Fishy riddles / by Katy Hall and Lisa Eisenberg;
pictures by Simms Taback.   p.   cm. — (Puffin easy-to-read)
Summary: A collection of simple riddles about fish such as
"Why are fish so smart? They are always in schools."
ISBN 0-14-036546-X
1. Riddles, Juvenile. 2. Fishes—Juvenile humor.
[1. Riddles. 2. Fishes—Wit and humor.]
I. Eisenberg, Lisa. II. Taback, Simms, ill. III. Title. IV. Series.
PN6371.5.H348   1993
818'.5402—dc20   93-6551   CIP   AC

Puffin® and Easy-to-Read® are registered trademarks of Penguin Books USA Inc.
Printed in the United States of America

Reading Level 2.4

Thanks, Jean
To the little minnows, Leigh and Kate
L.E. and K.H.

For Naomi and Russell Paul
S.T.

Why are fish so smart?

They are always in schools.

What does an octopus wear
on a cold day?

A coat of arms!

What is a knight's
favorite fish?

A swordfish.

Where do fish keep their money?

In the river bank!

10

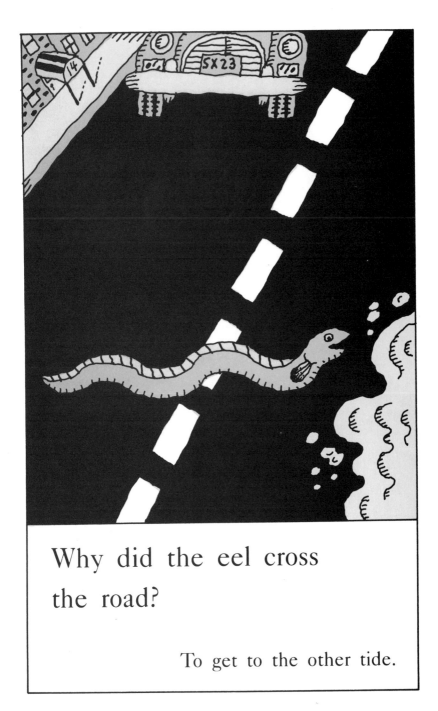

Why did the eel cross
the road?

To get to the other tide.

What did the boy octopus
say to the girl octopus?

I want to hold
your hand, hand, hand,
hand, hand, hand, hand, hand!

Where do fish come from?

Finland.

Where do sharks
come from?

Sharkago!

What TV game show
do fish like best?

Name That Tuna!

What did Cinderella
Dolphin wear to the ball?

Glass flippers!

What day of the week
do fish hate?

Fryday!

How do you keep fish
from smelling?

Hold their noses!

18

Which side of a fish has
the most scales?

The outside!

If a hungry shark
is after you,
what should you feed it?

Jawbreakers!

Have you ever seen
a fish cry?

No, but I have seen
whales blubber!

What is the best way
to talk to a shark?

Long-distance!

What did the sea say when
the plane flew over it?

Nothing.
It just waved.

What do you call
a frightened skin diver?

Chicken of the Sea!

Why are fishermen
so stingy?

Because their job
makes them sell fish!

How can you make
a whale float?

Two scoops of ice cream,
some root beer,
and a whale.

Why did the dog jump
into the river?

It wanted to chase
the catfish!

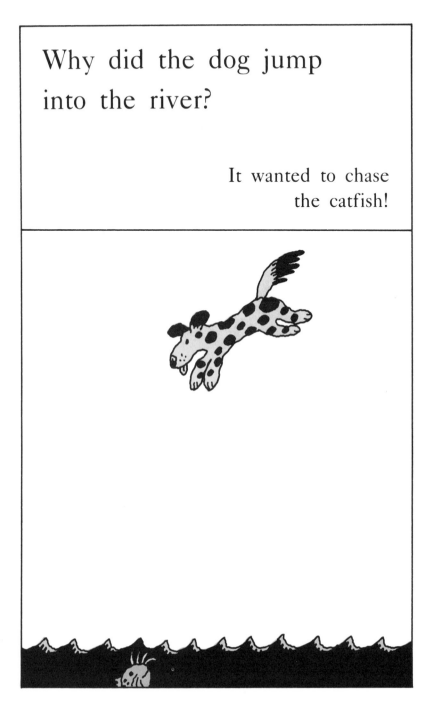

What did the cat become
when he jumped
into the river?

Wet.

What kind of ice cream
do sharks like?

Shark-o-lat!

What do whales have
that no other sea animals
have?

Baby whales!

What do whales like to eat with peanut butter?

Jellyfish!

What kind of sharks make good carpenters?

Hammerheads!

What did the fish do
when his piano sounded
funny?

He called
the piano tuna!

What bug loves skin diving?

A mosquito!

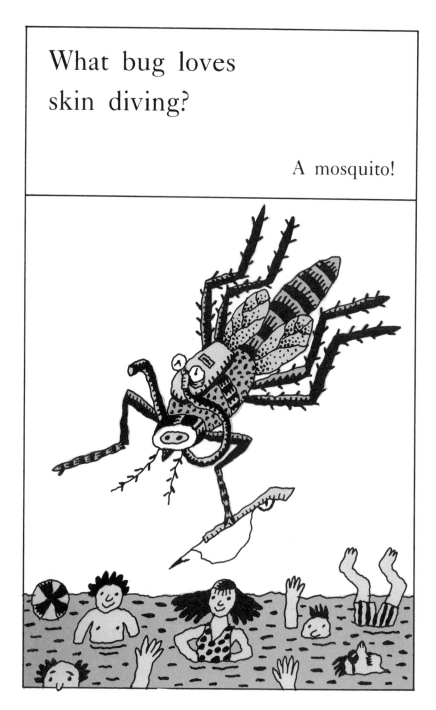

What do you call someone who sticks his right hand into a shark's mouth?

Lefty!

What do you get when you cross a math teacher and a crab?

Snappy answers!

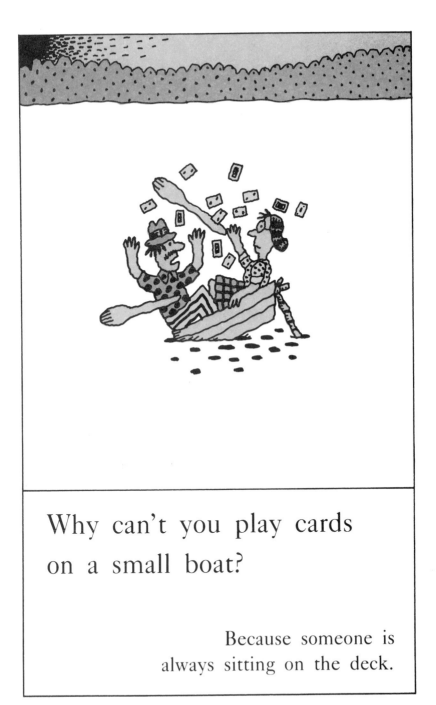

Why can't you play cards
on a small boat?

Because someone is
always sitting on the deck.

If you see a tuna being chased by a dozen sharks, what time is it?

Twelve after one.

What puts white lines
on the ocean?

Ocean liners.

What happened to Ray
when he was caught
by the giant squid?

He became X-Ray.

Why was the swordfish's
nose eleven inches
long?

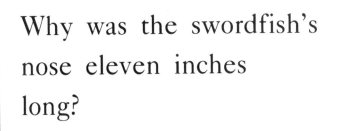

Because
if it were twelve inches long,
it would be a foot!

What hobby does a shark
like best?

Anything he can sink
his teeth into!

Who is the most famous
shark writer?

William Sharkspeare!

How do you tune a fish?

With its scales.

Why should you never swim
on a full stomach?

It's easier
to swim in water!

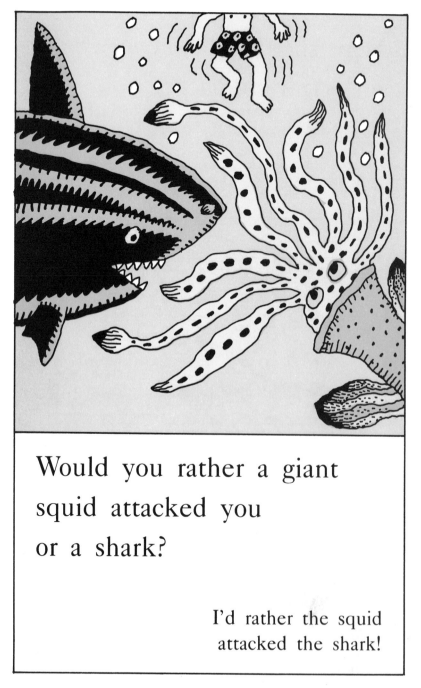

Would you rather a giant
squid attacked you
or a shark?

I'd rather the squid
attacked the shark!

What fish has
the most money?

A loan shark.

What would you get
if you crossed a cow
and a tadpole?

A bullfrog!